# The Cat that Went WOOF!

A humorous story
in a familiar setting

First published in 2004 by
Franklin Watts
338 Euston Road
London
NW1 3BH

Franklin Watts Australia
Level 17 / 207 Kent Street
Sydney
NSW 2000

Text © Martyn Beardsley 2004
Illustration © Lisa Smith 2004

A CIP catalogue record for this book is available
from the British Library.

ISBN 978 0 7496 5778 9

**Series Editor:** Jackie Hamley
**Series Advisors:** Dr Barrie Wade, Dr Hilary Minns
**Design:** Peter Scoulding


Printed in China


Franklin Watts is a division of
Hachette Children's Books.

# The Cat that Went
# WOOF!

Written by
## Martyn Beardsley

Illustrated by
## Lisa Smith

W
FRANKLIN WATTS
LONDON·SYDNEY

### Martyn Beardsley
"I love writing and reading stories. I like spooky stories best. I also like football and other sports. I hope you enjoy the book!"

### Lisa Smith
"I love to draw. I have been drawing all my life. I like to draw animals best. I hope you will have fun with Jack, Tiger and Patch."

Tiger lived with Jack.

They were the best of friends.

Then along came Patch.
Everything changed.

Everyone laughed when
Patch barked.

They patted his head when he
wagged his tail.

So Tiger decided she would learn to bark.

Then everyone would laugh and pat her head!

"WOOF!" said Tiger.

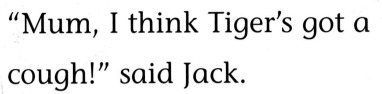

"Mum, I think Tiger's got a cough!" said Jack.

14

"WOOF! WOOF!" said Tiger
when the post arrived.

16

"Mum, I think Tiger's swallowed a letter!" said Jack.

19

They took Tiger to see the vet.

"What's wrong?" asked the vet.

"She doesn't sound very well,"
said Jack.

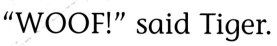

"WOOF!" said Tiger.

"I see!" said the vet.

"Do you have any other pets?"
asked the vet.

29

"MIAOW!" said Tiger.

"MIOOF!" said Patch.

31

# Notes for parents and teachers

READING CORNER has been structured to provide maximum support for new readers. The stories may be used by adults for sharing with young children. Primarily, however, the stories are designed for newly independent readers, whether they are reading these books in bed at night, or in the reading corner at school or in the library.

Starting to read alone can be a daunting prospect. READING CORNER helps by providing visual support and repeating words and phrases, while making reading enjoyable. These books will develop confidence in the new reader, and encourage a love of reading that will last a lifetime!

If you are reading this book with a child, here are a few tips:

**1.** Make reading fun! Choose a time to read when you and the child are relaxed and have time to share the story.

**2.** Encourage children to reread the story, and to retell the story in their own words, using the illustrations to remind them what has happened.

**3.** Give praise! Remember that small mistakes need not always be corrected.

READING CORNER covers three grades of early reading ability, with three levels at each grade. Each level has a certain number of words per story, indicated by the number of bars on the spine of the book, to allow you to choose the right book for a young reader:

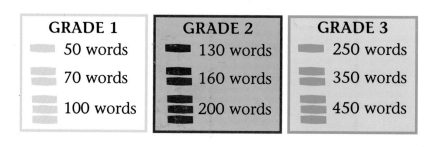

| GRADE 1 | GRADE 2 | GRADE 3 |
|---------|---------|---------|
| 50 words | 130 words | 250 words |
| 70 words | 160 words | 350 words |
| 100 words | 200 words | 450 words |